BATTLING COVID-19
Healthcare HEROES
Medical Workers Take On COVID-19

RACHAEL L. THOMAS

Checkerboard Library

An Imprint of Abdo Publishing
abdobooks.com

abdobooks.com

Published by Abdo Publishing, a division of ABDO, PO Box 398166, Minneapolis, Minnesota 55439. Copyright © 2021 by Abdo Consulting Group, Inc. International copyrights reserved in all countries. No part of this book may be reproduced in any form without written permission from the publisher. Checkerboard Library™ is a trademark and logo of Abdo Publishing.

Printed in the United States of America, North Mankato, Minnesota
102020
012021

THIS BOOK CONTAINS RECYCLED MATERIALS

Design: Sarah DeYoung, Mighty Media, Inc.
Production: Mighty Media, Inc.
Editor: Jessica Rusick
Cover Photograph: Shutterstock Images
Interior Photographs: Alamy, p. 13; AP Images, p. 27; Benjamin Slane/Milwaukee VA Medical Center/Flickr, p. 29; The National Guard/Flickr, p. 17; Ronen Tivony/AP Images, pp. 7 (top), 15; Sgt. 1st Class Ben Houtkooper/The National Guard/Flickr, p. 6 (bottom); Shutterstock Images, pp. 5, 6, 7, 9, 11, 19, 23, 24, 25; Spc. Jovi Prevot/Mississippi National Guard/Flickr, p. 21
Design Elements: Shutterstock Images

Library of Congress Control Number: 2020940243

Publisher's Cataloging-in-Publication Data
Names: Thomas, Rachael L., author.
Title: Healthcare heroes: medical workers take on COVID-19 / by Rachael L. Thomas
Other title: medical workers take on COVID-19
Description: Minneapolis, Minnesota : Abdo Publishing, 2021 | Series: Battling COVID-19 | Includes online resources and index
Identifiers: ISBN 9781532194283 (lib. bdg.) | ISBN 9781098213640 (ebook)
Subjects: LCSH: COVID-19 (Disease)--Juvenile literature. | Medical personnel--Juvenile literature. | Physicians--Juvenile literature. | Nurses--Juvenile literature. | Volunteers--Juvenile literature.
Classification: DDC 610.69--dc23

Contents

Healthcare Heroes 4
Timeline 6
Care and Concerns 8
Constant Exposure 10
PPE Shortage 12
Difficult Work 16
Protecting Loved Ones 18
Supporting Heroes 20
Global Impact 24
Ongoing Struggles 26
Heroes of the Pandemic 28
Glossary 30
Online Resources 31
Index 32

Healthcare Heroes

In late 2019, several people in Wuhan, China, became sick with a mysterious illness. Scientists soon discovered that the disease was caused by a new coronavirus. The disease was later named COVID-19.

Within months, COVID-19 spread to countries around the world. On March 11, 2020, the **World Health Organization (WHO)** declared COVID-19 a **pandemic**. To slow the spread of the disease, large public events were canceled. Schools and businesses closed. And, many governments asked people to stay at home.

But some people could not stay at home. Medical workers had to treat patients **infected** with COVID-19. Nurses, doctors, and other healthcare professionals spent long hours fighting the disease. They risked catching COVID-19 themselves. Healthcare heroes put their lives on the line to help others.

WHAT IS A CORONAVIRUS?

Coronaviruses are a large group of viruses that cause **respiratory** illnesses. Most coronaviruses exist only in animals. However, several have spread from animals to humans. The coronavirus discovered in Wuhan is called severe acute respiratory syndrome coronavirus 2 (SARS-CoV-2). It causes a disease called coronavirus disease 2019, or COVID-19. COVID-19 spreads when saliva droplets pass from person to person. This can happen when someone coughs, sneezes, sings, breathes, or talks. Most people with COVID-19 do not suffer serious **symptoms**. But some people develop life-threatening problems. Because of this, the virus is viewed as a threat to world health.

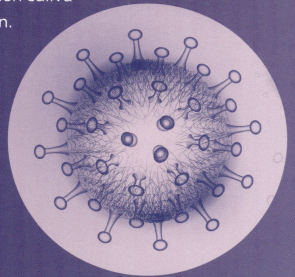

TIMELINE

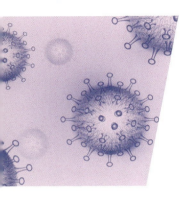

LATE 2019
People in Wuhan, China, become sick with COVID-19.

MARCH 11, 2020
The World Health Organization (WHO) declares COVID-19 a pandemic.

MID-MARCH 2020
Some US hospitals begin canceling nonemergency surgeries to focus on treating COVID-19 patients.

JANUARY 21, 2020
The United States reports its first case of COVID-19.

MARCH 19, 2020
The WHO advises medical workers on what personal protective equipment (PPE) to wear when treating patients with COVID-19.

FEBRUARY 29, 2020
The United States has 15 reported cases of COVID-19.

LATE MARCH 2020
Many US hospitals face shortages of PPE. Nurses in several US cities protest the lack of PPE.

APRIL 1, 2020
The United States has more than 210,000 cases of COVID-19.

LATE APRIL 2020
Some states begin to lift stay-at-home orders as COVID-19 cases decline.

EARLY OCTOBER 2020
More than 200,000 Americans have died from COVID-19.

APRIL 15, 2020
At least 9,200 US medical workers have been infected with COVID-19.

Care and Concerns

As COVID-19 spread around the world, experts learned how it affected people. Most people with COVID-19 had mild **symptoms**. They recovered without going to a hospital. But others had serious symptoms. These included difficulty breathing and organ failure. These people needed care from medical workers to recover.

Healthcare workers cared for COVID-19 patients in several ways. They provided medicines and other treatments to ease symptoms. In serious cases, COVID-19 care also included the use of a ventilator. This is a machine that helps a patient breathe.

The United States reported its first case of COVID-19 on January 21, 2020. By the end of February, the country had 15 reported cases. Some medical professionals expected these case numbers to increase rapidly in the following months. They worried that US hospitals were unprepared to handle a surge of COVID-19 patients.

Many hospitals around the country were already full of patients. So, they would not have space to take on COVID-19 patients.

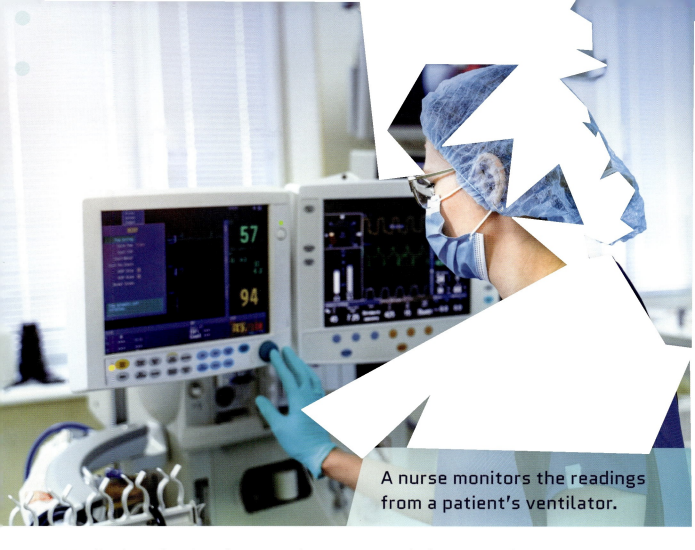

A nurse monitors the readings from a patient's ventilator.

Medical professionals were also concerned about ventilator **shortages**. Without ventilators, hospitals could not treat very sick COVID-19 patients.

Constant Exposure

By March 18, the United States had more than 7,000 reported COVID-19 cases. This number was doubling every few days. That month, many US governors issued stay-at-home orders. These orders were designed to slow the spread of COVID-19.

State leaders asked people to stay at home as much as possible. In public, people practiced social distancing. This meant staying at least six feet (2 m) apart from others in public. **Nonessential** businesses also closed. These included hair salons, movie theaters, and department stores.

Hospitals remained open. Many became overwhelmed as more people became sick with COVID-19. In mid-March, several hospitals began canceling nonemergency **surgeries**. That way, medical workers could focus on treating COVID-19 patients.

STEM CONNECTION

A person can get COVID-19 when droplets containing the SARS-CoV-2 virus enter the body. These droplets enter through the nose or mouth. The number of virus droplets in a person's body is called a viral load. The more virus droplets in a person's body, the higher the viral load. Some medical workers were exposed to the SARS-CoV-2 virus every day. So over time, they developed high viral loads. High viral loads of SARS-CoV-2 can make COVID-19 **symptoms** worse. So, medical workers were at greater risk of developing a serious case of COVID-19.

PPE Shortage

COVID-19 infections were spreading easily from person to person. So on March 19, the **WHO** advised medical workers on what personal protective equipment (PPE) to wear when treating COVID-19 patients. Medical workers wear PPE to protect themselves and their patients from infection. To treat COVID-19 patients, medical workers needed lots of PPE. This included medical gowns, gloves, and face masks. They also needed eye protection. This included goggles or face shields.

Most PPE is meant to be used once and thrown away. So, medical workers need a constant supply. Before the COVID-19 **pandemic**, many hospitals kept extra supplies of PPE. However, these quickly ran out as COVID-19 cases increased.

By late March, many US hospitals faced PPE **shortages**. One reason for the shortage was a low national supply. The United States **imported** some of its PPE from other countries. But these countries needed more PPE for their own healthcare workers during the pandemic. So, many countries stopped selling PPE

West Virginia Army National Guard members wear full PPE as they arrive to help with testing at a nursing home.

to the United States. Many US companies also make PPE. But they could not produce enough PPE to meet demand.

Because of the PPE **shortage**, masks and gowns became hard to find. So, some medical workers reused these items. Other workers wore scarves in place of masks and trash bags in place of gowns.

These solutions were not enough. Reused PPE is not as effective as fresh PPE. Without proper PPE, medical workers risked spreading COVID-19 to other patients. And, they risked catching the disease themselves.

In late March, nurses in several US cities protested the lack of PPE. They demanded that the US government send PPE to hospitals. Their protests helped raise public awareness about PPE shortages. In response, people across the nation **donated** spare face masks and gloves to hospitals. Others sewed masks for healthcare workers. These donations didn't make up for the PPE shortage. However, they helped contribute to the fight against COVID-19.

Medical workers in California protest PPE shortages.

Difficult Work

By April 1, the United States had more than 210,000 reported cases of COVID-19. This was more cases than any other country had. Many US COVID-19 cases were in New York. By April 9, the state had 150,000 cases. Thousands of New Yorkers were hospitalized with COVID-19 each day.

Most of New York's cases were in or near New York City. Medical workers and hospitals there were overwhelmed. Some doctors and nurses worked 16-hour shifts to treat all the new cases. Hospitals ran out of room as patients filled **intensive care units**. **Field hospitals** helped with patient overflow.

Hospitals in New York City and around the country also faced ventilator **shortages**. Medical workers sometimes had to choose which patients received ventilators. These were difficult, heartbreaking choices. Access to a ventilator often meant the difference between life and death.

Medical staff also had the difficult job of comforting very sick patients. In April, thousands of COVID-19 patients were dying

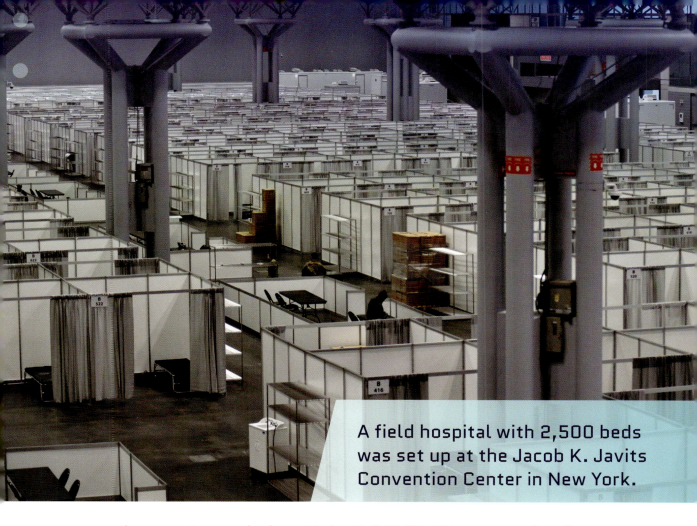

A field hospital with 2,500 beds was set up at the Jacob K. Javits Convention Center in New York.

across the country each day. To limit COVID-19's spread, family members were not always allowed to visit their sick loved ones. Medical workers were often the only people in the room when COVID-19 patients passed away.

Protecting Loved Ones

By mid-April, COVID-19 was infecting tens of thousands of Americans each day. Many doctors and nurses felt scared for their personal health. By April 15, at least 9,200 US medical workers had gotten COVID-19. However, many states did not track what jobs those infected with COVID-19 held. So, the number of infections among medical workers was likely much higher.

Many healthcare workers worried about infecting their loved ones with COVID-19. After their shifts, some practiced social distancing at home. This meant staying six feet (2 m) away from family members. Others temporarily moved to a different home to **isolate**. But not all medical workers had another place to stay.

To help, the American Hotel and Lodging Association founded the Hospitality for Hope initiative in March. The project provided free hotel rooms to healthcare workers. The hotel rooms ensured workers would not spread the virus to loved ones. In April, more

A doctor isolated from his family stops by his house to visit his children.

than 15,000 hotels volunteered to take part in Hospitality for Hope. The hotels chosen were close to hospitals. This made it easier for workers to travel to and from their shifts.

Supporting Heroes

Hospitality for Hope showed gratitude for healthcare professionals. In addition, people around the world showed their gratitude in many ways. Some celebrated medical workers beginning or ending their hospital shifts. Each day, people clapped and cheered from windows and balconies nearby hospitals.

Other people hung signs and banners in their windows supporting healthcare workers. Children drew colorful sidewalk chalk drawings thanking doctors and nurses. In many cities, buildings and other landmarks were lit up in blue. This color represents the medical industry.

Several art museums also showed their support for healthcare workers. They did so by sharing healthcare-themed artwork on social media. These posts used the hashtag #MuseumsThankHealthHeroes. Contributors to the social media campaign included the Whitney Museum of American Art in New York. The High Museum of Art in Atlanta, Georgia, also joined.

Members of the Mississippi National Guard thank healthcare workers for their work during the pandemic.

As COVID-19 cases increased, more states opened **field hospitals**. One state was California. Medical workers there were already busy treating patients in regular hospitals. So, the state recruited people such as retired doctors and nurses for the California Health **Corps**. This group helped staff field hospitals in the state. And, it provided nonurgent medical care to California residents. This relieved pressure on local hospitals.

Businesses and organizations found other ways to help medical workers. Some restaurants cooked meals for overworked hospital staff. During long shifts, many medical workers were too busy to make or order food. Food **donations** ensured these workers did not go hungry.

The organization Slice Out Hunger also focused on food. In March, it launched a project called Pizza vs. **Pandemic**. The campaign sent pizza to medical workers treating COVID-19 patients. In its first seven months, Pizza vs. Pandemic delivered 32,600 pizzas to healthcare workers.

Medical staff appreciated these acts of kindness. Many reported a boost in **morale** from the donations and support. Medical workers also reminded people to help by following

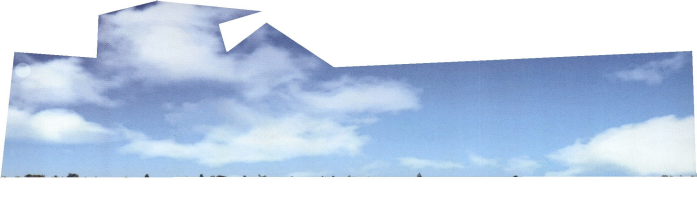

The US Navy sent hospital ships to help with the crisis. USNS *Comfort* went to New York City. USNS *Mercy* (shown) went to Los Angeles, California.

stay-at-home orders. That way, COVID-19 cases would go down. By late April, stay-at-home orders appeared to be working. In several states, the number of new COVID-19 cases was slowly declining. However, medical workers still faced challenges ahead.

Global Impact

UNITED KINGDOM

On April 5, United Kingdom prime minister Boris Johnson was hospitalized with COVID-19. Later that month, Johnson's partner gave birth to a baby boy. The couple named their baby Wilfred Lawrie Nicholas Johnson. The name Nicholas honored two doctors who had helped Johnson recover from COVID-19.

FRANCE

On April 11, chefs Alan Taudon and Christian Le Squer cooked for employees at a hospital in Paris, France. These chefs ran expensive restaurants in Paris. They prepared fancy meals for hungry hospital workers.

CHINA

On April 7, the Shanghai Disney Resort theme park in China lit up its Enchanted Storybook Castle to honor medical workers. The castle was illuminated with the words for "thank you" in different languages.

GREECE

In late April, orchestras performed for medical staff and patients outside several hospitals in Greece. The performances were meant to bring healthcare workers peace in the middle of long shifts.

Ongoing Struggles

In late April, some states began to lift stay-at-home orders. For hard-hit states, the worst seemed to have passed. Each day, fewer people were being hospitalized with COVID-19.

But the **pandemic** was far from over. In July 2020, cases increased again in several states. These included Texas and Florida.

As cases increased, medical workers continued to face struggles. Some were physical. Many medical workers had bruises on their cheeks and foreheads. These were from wearing tight face masks all day. Other struggles were emotional. Medical workers had spent months working under extreme pressure. They had seen many patients suffer.

STEM CONNECTION

Some mental health experts worried that medical workers might suffer post-traumatic **stress** disorder (PTSD) from treating COVID-19 patients. PTSD is a mental health condition. It affects those who have experienced something extremely stressful or frightening. **Symptoms** of PTSD include nightmares and anxiety.

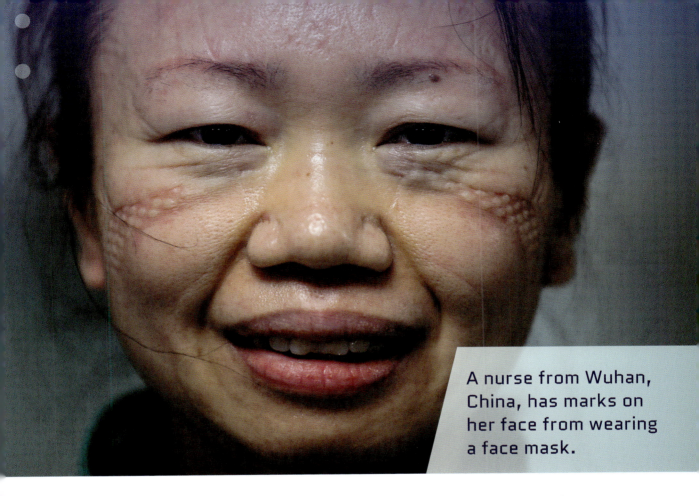

A nurse from Wuhan, China, has marks on her face from wearing a face mask.

Experts worried how COVID-19 would affect medical workers' mental health. Studies from Wuhan showed that healthcare workers had experienced **depression** and anxiety during the **pandemic**. Some US hospitals had programs to help medical workers through mental health struggles. But it would take time for medical workers to heal.

Heroes of the Pandemic

In September, COVID-19 infections rose once again in several states. These included Texas, Alabama, and Arizona. Medical workers across the country struggled to treat patients. Many hospitals still had limited staff and supplies.

By early October, more than 7 million Americans had been infected with COVID-19. More than 200,000 had died. But new deaths were declining across the country. This was partly because medical workers better understood how to treat patients. New medicines also helped patients recover faster.

Healthcare workers had saved many lives. But they had a long road ahead. Many hospitals still had PPE **shortages**. And, experts **predicted** COVID-19 cases could increase in the winter.

US medical workers faced an uncertain future. But one thing was certain. As new challenges arose, healthcare heroes would have the support of the nation behind them.

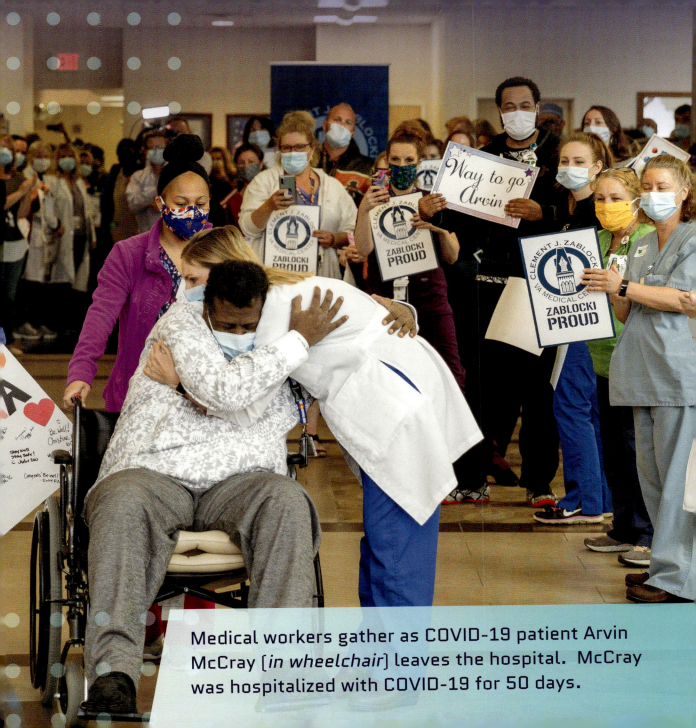

Medical workers gather as COVID-19 patient Arvin McCray (*in wheelchair*) leaves the hospital. McCray was hospitalized with COVID-19 for 50 days.

Glossary

corps—a group of people that has a certain function.

depression—a state of feeling sad or dejected.

donate—to give. A donation is something that is given.

field hospital—a temporary hospital that provides emergency care to the sick or wounded.

gratitude—the state of being grateful or thankful.

import—to bring in goods from another country for sale or use.

infection—an unhealthy condition caused by something harmful, such as a virus. If something has an infection, it is infected.

intensive care unit—a department of a hospital for very sick patients.

isolate—to separate from others.

morale—the enthusiasm and loyalty a person or group feels about a task or job.

nonessential—something that is not important or necessary.

pandemic—worldwide spread of a disease that can affect most people.

predict—to guess something ahead of time on the basis of observation, experience, or reasoning.

respiratory—having to do with the system of organs involved with breathing.

shortage—a lack of something that is needed.

stress—a physical, chemical, or emotional factor that causes bodily or mental strain. It may be involved in causing some diseases. Something that causes stress is stressful.

surgery—the treating of sickness or injury by cutting into and repairing body parts.

symptom—a noticeable change in the normal working of the body. A symptom indicates or accompanies disease, sickness, or another malfunction.

World Health Organization (WHO)—an agency of the United Nations that works to maintain and improve the health of people around the world.

Online Resources

To learn more about the COVID-19 pandemic, please visit **abdobooklinks.com** or scan this QR code. These links are routinely monitored and updated to provide the most current information available.

Index

Alabama, 28
American Hotel and Lodging Association, 18
Arizona, 28

bruises, 26

California, 22
California Health Corps, 22
cases, 4, 8, 10, 16, 18, 22, 23, 24, 26, 28
China, 4, 5, 25, 27
closures, 4, 10
COVID-19 symptoms, 5, 8, 11

deaths, 16, 17, 28
doctors, 4, 16, 18, 20, 22, 24
donations, 14, 22

field hospitals, 16, 22
Florida, 26
France, 24

Georgia, 20
Greece, 25

High Museum of Art, 20
Hospitality for Hope, 18, 19, 20

Johnson, Boris, 24

medicines, 8, 28
mental health, 26, 27
#MuseumsThankHealthHeroes, 20

New York, 16, 20
nurses, 4, 14, 16, 18, 20

patient care, 4, 8, 9, 10, 12, 16, 17, 18, 22, 28
personal protective equipment (PPE), 12, 14, 26, 28
Pizza vs. Pandemic, 22
protests, 14

SARS-CoV-2 virus, 4, 5, 11, 18
Slice Out Hunger, 22
social distancing, 10, 18
stay-at-home orders, 4, 10, 23, 26
supply shortages, 9, 12, 14, 16, 28

Texas, 26, 28

United Kingdom, 24
United States, 8, 10, 12, 14, 16, 18, 20, 23, 28

ventilators, 8, 9, 16

Whitney Museum of American Art, 20
World Health Organization (WHO), 4, 12